coney \\ˈkō-nē\\ n [ME *conies*, pl. fr. OF *conis*, fr. L. *cuniculus*] 1a: *RABBIT*; esp: the European rabbit b: rabbit fur 2: *DUPE*

To my Coney, with lots of lettuce.

Clarion Books
a Houghton Mifflin Company imprint
215 Park Avenue South, New York, NY 10003
Text and Illustrations copyright © 1992 by Paul Rátz de Tagyos

Library of Congress Cataloging-in-Publication Data

Rátz de Tagyos, Paul.
A coney tale / written and illustrated by Paul Rátz de Tagyos.
p.   cm.
Summary: The inhabitants of a rabbit village in
seventeenth-century Flanders discover the biggest carrot in
the world and try to dig it up.
ISBN 0-395-58834-0
[1. Rabbits — Fiction.   2. Carrots — Fiction.   3.
Flanders — Fiction.]   I. Title.
PZ7.R19395Co   1992
[E] — dc20   90-27787   CIP   AC

HOR 10 9 8 7 6 5 4 3 2 1

Paul Rátz de Tagyos

A Coney Tale

CLARION BOOKS • NEW YORK

In the seventeenth century in the windy part of Europe, then called Flanders, there was a little village known as Conage. That's where our coney tale comes from.

Conage was a quiet farming community where all the little coneys worked together and helped one another. There were no battles or disputes because there was nothing to fight over. There was plenty of food. Coneys love nothing better than feeding. Not much has changed about that for hundreds of years.

Though farming was the main activity in Conage, the town boasted a pad repair shop,

an ear care center,

a fancy chocolate shop,

and even an old-time pellet maker. Conage also had a little town council house.

Inside, the councillor coneys met to decide on community matters, such as which streets would get their mud holes filled, and when to repair the windmills.

Across from the council house was the village square. It was the central meeting place. The coneys would gather there for games and talking, storytelling and playing, and of course feeding. The square had gravel paths and flowers. There were some benches and a statue of a great coney king. But the most striking thing in the square was a big tree.

This tree was the pride of Conage. It was said to be hundreds and hundreds of years old. Coneys would come from miles around just to look at and sit in the shade of the biggest tree in coney Flanders.

One sunny morning a village coney named Holbun the Elder was instructing his son, Holbun the Younger, in the fine art of archery. He set up a target in the square and showed little Holbun how to hold the bow, how to draw back the arrow, and how to take aim, making sure no one was near when they let their arrows fly. However, Holbun never hit his mark. The arrows sailed over and around the target and landed at the base of the biggest tree.

Holbun the Younger went to gather the arrows. "They're stuck," he called.

Sure enough, his father found them hard to pull up. "Caught in the tree roots," he said, huffing. When the arrows came up, each one had a chunk of root stuck on it, and these chunks were bright orange. "Strange," mused Holbun the Elder. "I've never seen tree roots this color before." He plucked a chunk off an arrow and smelled it. Then he tasted it.

"Impossible!" he said. "It can't be!" He plucked off the rest of the chunks and put them in his apron pocket. "Quick, hop with me!" he told his bun son. They hopped across the square at top speed and burst into the council house.

Holbun thrust the orange tree chips at the councillors. "Eat these!" he ordered.

No coney needs to be asked twice to eat something. They ate the chips. "Well?" they said, bewildered.

"What did it *taste* like?" asked a very excited Holbun.

The councillor coneys all looked at one another. "Carrots, of course," the head councillor replied.

"Come with us! Immediately!" cried Holbun. Grumbling and muttering, the councillors followed him into the square.

At the base of the great tree, Holbun whipped out his pocket knife, chipped off little chunks of tree root, and handed them around. The councillors ate their chunks and looked at one another in disbelief. "Why, this isn't a tree at all," said one of the councillor coneys.

"Why, it's...it's..." stammered another.

"It's the biggest carrot in the world!" cried little Holbun. "Let's dig it up!"

"We can't do that," one of the councillors protested. "This tree is hundreds of years old. Why, it's the pride of Conage."

Another councillor added, "It would be a crime to dig up such a glorious tree — or carrot."

"But wait a minute," little Holbun said. "We are coneys, after all. Coneys are supposed to dig up carrots."

"And think of all the coneys it will feed," added Holbun the Elder.

That did it. Feeding was close to the head councillor's heart. "Very well," he declared. "We shall dig up the giant carrot." Everyone applauded.

The Holbuns hurried to spread the good news. That night, in all the hutches in Conage, no one talked about anything but the giant carrot. Early the next morning, even before sunrise, all the coneys came with little shovels and buckets to help dig up the biggest carrot in the world.

It soon became obvious that shovels and buckets were not enough, so they built giant scoopers. These scoopers were sort of like catapults, but upside down. They made the digging go faster, but there were problems. Giant gobs of soil flying through the air had to land somewhere, and they did....

... But not always in the best places.

Down in the hole the coneys rigged a system of pulleys to hoist up the containers of soil. The digging (a natural bunny habit) went on for months. News of the excavation spread across Flanders. Coneys from all over came to watch and help, not to mention eat.

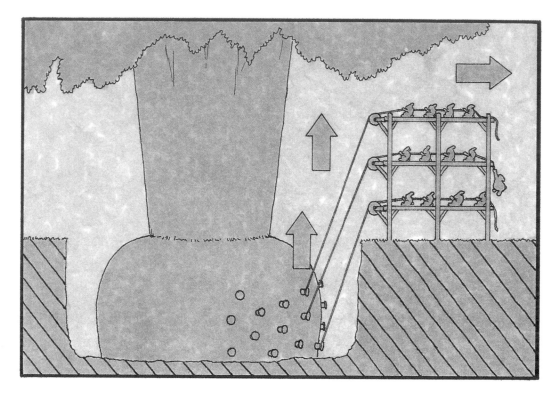

Finally the hole looked deep enough. Pegs were driven into the carrot, and ropes were attached all around. Armies of coneys standing on scaffolding were ready to pull on the ropes. The head councillor stood on a box and shouted, "Pull! Pull! Pull!"

Hundreds of coneys pulled with all their furry might. And they pulled again, hopper pads shuffling on the ground. The Biggest Carrot in the World trembled ever so little, but did not budge. Harrumph! Now what? They tried and tried, but the carrot would not move.

The coneys tried to figure out what to do. Coneys are better at feeding than at thinking. There was a lot of head scratching and pacing back and forth. Some forgot what they were supposed to be thinking about.

Little Holbun, feeling discouraged, went for a short hop to the shore. He hopped along the dike wall and felt the wind against his fur. The air smelled good. He looked out at the water and the boats...the trees and the sky...the windmills all in a row. And suddenly he knew how to pull up the giant carrot!

Holbun quick-hopped home with his wonderful idea. His whole family went with him to the council house, where the councillors immediately started drawing up plans to make little Holbun's idea a reality. Builders began building it the very next day, right on top of the scaffolding.

At last the idea was ready to be tested. Because he had thought it up, Holbun the Younger was chosen to give the signal. "You must yell very loudly, so all can hear," said the head councillor.

Holbun the Younger nodded solemnly, took a deep breath, and yelled, "Ready...*set*...PULL!" And the coneys pulled. The wood creaked and the ropes tightened, but that was all.

Then a gust of wind came, the kind that Flanders is famous for. A worker coney attached the big ropes to the main turning shaft. The coneys kept pulling and the wind kept blowing.

The whole scaffold creaked, and the big ropes strained. Nothing happened. After a moment a deep rumbling was heard and felt, and the carrot began to move. With new hope the coneys pulled harder than ever. A stronger gust of wind, a harder pull, and the earth seemed to open up. With a thunderous roar, the carrot pulled free with such force that it went soaring through the air, taking all the coneys with it.

The carrot landed in a farmer's field just outside the village. No coneys were hurt, as they are generally a rather bouncy group.

After getting up and dusting off, all the coneys went speeding to the giant carrot. There was a moment of silence. They were awestruck. No coney had ever dared to imagine a carrot so huge, so terrific, so magnificent.

Then, without a word, as if in response to a silent signal, the whole vast crowd of coneys dove at the giant carrot and started feeding and feeding and feeding. It was a feeding frenzy unlike anything seen in Conage before or since.

In due course, the giant hole left by the carrot was filled with water and turned into a public fountain. The Holbun family was paraded through the streets of Conage, and the whole population turned out to applaud and cheer.

They say that thousands of coneys fed for months on the carrot that had been the biggest tree in coney Flanders. And they say that the carrot was so big, it reached through the earth to China, on the other side of the world. Some say this is true, and some say it isn't. Coneys, though, they all believe, and that is why — to this day — they always look carefully at every big tree.